THEY BELONG TO THE GREAT KING.

Page 17.

The King's Messengers.

THE

KING'S MESSENGERS,

AN ALLEGORICAL TALE.

BY THE

REV. W. ADAMS, M. A.

FELLOW OF MERTON COLLEGE, OXFORD

AUTHOR OF

THE SHADOW OF THE CROSS.

Lay up for yourselves treasures in Heaven.—Matt, vi. 20

FROM THE LONDON EDITION,

WITH ENGRAVINGS EXECUTED BY W. HOWLAND

FROM ORIGINAL DESIGNS

BY WEIR.

EIGHTH AMERICAN EDITION.

NEW YORK:

GENERAL PROTESTANT EPISCOPAL S. S. UNION

and Church Book Society,

762 BROADWAY.

1858.

TO

CONSTANCE KNOLLYS

AND

HER BROTHERS

This Little Volume is Inscribed

BY

THEIR GODFATHER

THE AUTHOR.

Advertisement.

THE following tale differs, in some respects, both in design and character, from the preceding allegories by the same author. It is not intended to give a general view of our state as Christians, but merely to bring forward, prominently and distinctly, a single Christian duty. In consequence of this, it involves very little of doctrinal teaching, while the allegorical meaning lies so completely on the surface, that the youngest child cannot fail to apprehend it. For both these reasons, any *explanatory* conversations have been considered unnecessary. But a conversation of a different character has been annexed, in order to obviate the misconstruction to which the dwelling on any one duty to the exclusion of others is always liable, and, at the same time, to apply and illustrate the truths conveyed in the story.

Bonchurch,
Dec. 26, 1847.

Introduction.

"HAS any one called during my absence?" inquired Mr. Mertoun of his nephew, Leonard, on returning home after his usual round of parochial visits.

"No one," replied the boy; "I have been with Mary in the garden, and if they had, I could not have helped seeing them."

"It is strange," said Mr. Mertoun, "are you quite sure there has been no one?"

"Quite sure," he answered, but presently added, correcting himself, "at least, no one of any consequence—only some poor man."

The tone in which the last words were uttered, no less than the answer itself, grated harshly on Mr. Mertoun's ear. "*Only some poor man!*" he repeated; "why, Leonard, do you say *only?* Might not ***his*** visit be of consequence?"

The boy looked confused, but endeavoured to justify his former reply, by saying, "Of consequence to himself, uncle, but I meant, of no consequence to you."

"Nay, my dear boy," replied Mr. Mertoun, "you now speak even more thoughtlessly than before. It could not have been the one without being the other also. Remember, that it can never be of more importance for the poor man to declare his wants than it is for those who have the means to relieve them. Do you think you understand me?"

"I believe, uncle, I do," he replied, thoughtfully. "You mean, as you told us on Sunday, that 'it is more blessed to give than to receive.'"

"Mr. Mertoun perceived from the reply, that he had awakened the train of reflection which he wished, and did not, at the time, pursue the conversation. But the words, "*only some poor man*," kept recurring painfully to his own mind. His nephew and niece had been with him but a few days, yet it was not the first time he had observed in them a want of sympathy for the poor. This was, perhaps, an almost necessary result of their having been brought up in London. No opportunity had been there afforded them of visiting the poor in their own homes. They had learned to look upon all beggars as impostors, and drew no distinction between real and pretended cases of distress. Thus, though in other respects they were loving and obedient children, and well grounded in the principles of the Christian faith, the numerous warnings in the Gospel concerning the danger of wealth, and its only safeguard, remained to them almost a dead letter.

It was with a view of remedying this defect, and bringing distinctly before them the important office assigned to the poor by our Blessed LORD, that on the evening of the above conversation their uncle told them the following story.

The King's Messengers.

CHAPTER I.

Largely Thou givest, gracious LORD,
Largely Thy gifts should be restored:
Freely Thou givest, and Thy word
Is "freely give."
He only who forgets to hoard,
Has learn'd to live.

CHRISTIAN YEAR.

THE city of Metœcia lay to the west of the dominions of a Great King. It was an ancient city, and had gradually become very large and populous. But the original settlers had been placed there in consequence of a rebellion against the King's authority; and a remarkable law continued to prevail among their descendants as a memorial of their crime. No one was allowed to remain in it above a certain number of years, and no one, when he left it, was permitted to take any portion of his property with him. This was called the law of Exile. The Great King had himself enacted it, and the citizens had no resource but submission. There was not even a fixed and definite period allotted for their stay. They were liable at any moment to receive the Royal Mandate. It came to them also one by one. As each was summoned to depart, his dearest friends could only accompany him as far as the gates of the city. And he was then stripped of all his possessions, and sent forth as an exile on his solitary journey.

Now, as the inhabitants of Metœcia were principally merchants, one would have imagined that such a law must have proved a source of perpetual disquietude and alarm. Yet this was not the case. Occasionally, indeed, when it was enforced against a very rich man, it would awaken sad thoughts in his companions, and cause them to mourn over the uncertainty of their wealth. But, for the most part, they all lived on in a false security. Every one fancied his possessions to be as really his own as though he had been able to retain them at will. Such a delusion may appear unaccountable; but, we must remember, that they had gradually become accustomed to the law, and for that reason it was lightly regarded by them or altogether forgotten.

The Great King, however, was full of compassion, and took much thought for the poor exiles, who were thus careless of themselves. He knew how dark and dreary was the wilderness that surrounded the city, and was unwilling that any should be left there to perish. He did not, indeed, reverse his original decree, but he did far more than this. He changed it from a punishment into a blessing. He offered to receive the exiles into a better and more glorious City than that from which he took them. If they rejected this offer the fault was their own. All the conditions on which it was made were very easy, and the King himself had promised to enable the citizens to perform them. But we need not dwell upon them all, for one alone which applied more especially to the wealthier merchants is brought before us by the present story.

In the city of Metœcia dwelt four brothers, Philargyr, Megacles, Euprepes, and Sophron. At the period at which I commence their history, the sentence of exile had lately been pronounced against their father. He had been a merchant of enormous wealth; and as, in accordance with the law, he was allowed to take nothing for his own wants, the whole of his vast possessions had fallen into the hands of his children. They had met in order to divide them. The room in which they assembled for this purpose was filled with the most costly furniture. The floor was covered with cloth of gold, which was now partially concealed by bales of yet more valuable merchandise, and heaps of precious stones which had been placed there, to await the choice of the brothers. Two sides of the apartment were hung with the most gorgeous tapestry, on the third was a window commanding an extensive view towards the west, while the wall opposite to the window was entirely covered by a spacious mirror, which reflected the various objects in the room itself and the street beyond.

But, in the midst of all this external splendour, a cloud sate on the countenance of each of the brothers. The departure of their father was too recent to allow them to forget the transitory character of the treasures which they were about to share. Let a few years pass, and each in his turn would be compelled to leave them, and go forth without money, without home, and without friends, into the dreary desert that lay around the city.

It was these thoughts which rendered them sad. They had never before felt the full burthen of the law of exile; they had been aware of its existence, for no citizen could be ignorant of it; but hitherto they had seen it, as it were, in the distance. It now seemed to meet them directly in their own path, and to force itself on their attention; so that the eldest brother did but echo the feelings of the rest when he said, "Of what profit is this enormous wealth? In the day of our banishment it will not purchase for us the delay of a single hour. How gladly would I barter the whole of it for some quiet dwelling-place, where we might remain in security for ever!"

He had not yet finished speaking, when his eyes were attracted by the mirror, which I have described as covering one side of the room. Some image appeared to be moving across it, which was not visible in the apartment itself. He pointed it out to his brothers, and it was clear from their anxious looks that they beheld it also. It was as the form of an old man. There was nothing in his appearance to excite terror, but every object as seen in the mirror was changed by his presence, His foot trod on the cloth of gold, and it became mouldering and worm-eaten: The hem of his garment swept against a table of solid ivory, and it fell crumbling into dust: while the bales of merchandise and precious stones lost their richness and splendour, as his cold eye rested upon them.

The brothers watched these signs with a sensation of chilling fear, and the eldest already repented his hasty words. For, in truth, in his inmost heart, he deeply loved the glittering wealth, and he was afraid lest the mysterious stranger might take it away, and give him in its stead the quiet dwelling for which he had asked.

At length it seemed to them that the image of the old man thus addressed them:—"Children, your wish is vain. You must not speak of bartering these treasures for a lasting home. They are not really yours; they belong to the Great King, whose subjects you are

Restore them to him now, and he will keep them for you, and in the day of your exile give them to you again. In this city they are worthless. See how even my slightest touch here causes them to decay. But in the King's palace they become incorruptible. I have no power over them there."

The brothers were yet more troubled at his words. They knew well that all the riches of Metœcia belonged to the Great King; but they were disquieted at the thought of restoring them to him again. A vague fear arose that the sentence of exile was about to be passed against themselves; and all, in some degree, shared the apprehensions of Philargyr. The old man appeared to read their thoughts, and thus replied to them:—

"Fear not; I am not now come to deprive you of your wealth. Hereafter, indeed, I shall return with the Royal Mandate, but in that hour you will both see and feel that I am near. To-day my voice comes to you from a distance, and it is but my reflected image that you behold. Yet I bear you a message from the Great King. You have wished to purchase for yourselves a lasting home; I have said that you cannot purchase it, because your riches are not your own; they belong to the Great King. You must trust them freely to his Messengers, without asking for a return; and he will store them up for you in his own palace, and, when you are driven from hence, will suffer you to dwell with his children in a Glorious City where the law of exile is unknown.

But beware lest you neglect this warning, and defraud the Great King of the riches committed to your trust; for if you refuse to give them to his Messengers, and either hoard them up or spend them on yourselves, you will have no treasure laid up for you in the Royal Palace, and the gates of the Glorious City will be closed against you for ever."

Now, there was nothing really new to the merchants in the old man's warning. The royal offers of pardon, and the dangers of the neglect of them, were well known in the city. But the inhabitants seldom spoke of them to one another, because they loved their riches and were unwilling to render obedience to the King's commands. The brothers had hitherto shared in the general feeling; and it was, perhaps, only because the remembrance of their father's departure was weighing heavily upon them that they had so long listened to the voice which now addressed them. It did not, indeed, seem to pass through their ears at all, but to fall at once inwardly on their hearts, and for the present they could not help regarding it. Yet all shrank from asking in what way they were to send their treasures to the Royal Palace. They were not, however, left in doubt. The reflection of the street in which their house stood was, as I have said, visible in the mirror. The figure of the old man now pointed towards it; and as he did so, the young merchants heard distinctly the words, "Behold the Messengers of the Great King!"

They followed the direction of his finger, and it seemed to them that the approach to their luxurious dwelling was now crowded with every form of disease and want. The poor, the maimed, and the blind, were there. Men who seemed stimulated to madness by famine, and little infants who could scarce crawl upon the ground, formed part of the same vast concourse. Still, as the old man pointed, their numbers went on increasing in every direction, until, as far as the eye could reach, every sign of wealth and luxury had disappeared, and in their stead was one universal scene of misery. Presently the shrieks of the dying, the cries of orphans, and the wailing of widows, rose in the air; and then, out of the tumult, the low solemn voice of the old man fell once more on the hearts of the brothers.

"These," he said, "and such as these, are the Messengers of the Great King. Numerous as they are, they will come to you in secret, and one by one. Trust them with your treasure, and it will be safe; they will bear it for you to the Royal Palace. The journey thither is long and dangerous; but if you are sincere in your wish to send it, the Great King will not suffer it to be lost. Only do not cause them to linger needlessly within the city walls; and let their departure be secret, lest the King's enemies should impede them on their way."

The form of the old man gradually disappeared as he ceased speaking; and the signs of his presence passed away;

the ivory table, the cloth of gold, and the heaps of precious stones, resumed the beauty and splendour which they had lost. The brothers once more breathed freely. Hitherto their eyes had been riveted by a kind of fascination on the mirror. They now looked anxiously around the apartment itself; but it had undergone no change. If the old man had trodden upon it, not one trace of his footsteps had been left. They then turned their eyes towards the window. The street presented its usual appearance; there was the busy throng hurrying hither and thither, and splendid equipages, and waggons laden with merchandise. But they saw nothing to remind them of the view presented by the mirror, save some few beggars who chanced to linger at their door. As Philargyr threw open the sash to inhale the fresh air, they eagerly asked the young merchants for alms; and there was not one who at that moment could refuse to give them; for the words of the stranger were fresh in their memory, and they felt every poor man to be a Messenger from the Great King.

The King's Messengers.

CHAPTER II.

CHRIST before thy door is waiting—
  Rouse thee, slave of earthly gold.
Lo, He comes, thy pomp abating,
  Hungry, thirsty, homeless, cold.

LYRA INNOCENTIUM

THE brothers were too deeply affected by the warning of the old man to proceed to the immediate division of their wealth. At one time, they even contemplated holding it in common, and consulted together on the best means of restoring it to the Great King. But from the first, their views differed so greatly, that they could agree on no settled plan. And, during the interval consumed in their discussions, their feelings underwent a partial change The words of the stranger seemed to lose their distinctness. Their riches recovered, in some degree, the value they had lost; and at length they reverted to their original plan of dividing them into four parts, so that each might take his own share, and do with it as he pleased.

Philargyr was entrusted with the division. Many months elapsed while he was absorbed in his calculations, and settling how large a portion he might appropriate to himself. During this time he was more than once interrupted by Messengers from the Great King. But their applications were in vain. He always returned the same answer, that, until the property was divided, no portion of it could be transmitted to the Royal Palace.

At length the division was made. The younger brothers were satisfied, though none were able to follow the calculations of Philargyr. Each had a share assigned to him, which, considering the shortness of their probable sojourn in the city, seemed inexhaustible, and each was left to follow his own course.

I proceed to give a brief sketch of their history.

The remarkable point in that of Philargyr, the eldest, was his utter forgetfulness, not only of the old man's warning, but of the law of the city in which he dwelt. Every act of his life appeared to set them at defiance. His one great object was to accumulate wealth. He neither trusted it to the King's Messengers, nor spent it in procuring the good-will of his fellow-citizens, but hoarded it up within the walls of his own house. There was no present gratification that he would not sacrifice, in the hope of adding to his possessions for future years. And this he did with the sentence of exile hanging over his head, and the positive certainty, that, when he left the city, he would not be allowed to take the smallest portion of them away.

I have already said, that the inhabitants of Metœcia lived, for the most part, in forgetfulness of the law of Exile. But the conduct of Philargyr appeared unaccountable even to the most thoughtless among them. He was supposed to be under the influence of a spell; and the following legend was commonly reported through the city:—

There had been, it was rumoured, a mine of gold communicating with the house of the departed merchant. Philargyr had taken possession of it, unknown to his brothers. This mine was haunted by an evil spirit, who had beguiled him by specious offers of assistance. For a time they had laboured together; but the evil spirit, while pretending to work out the precious ore, had changed the mine into a dungeon, and bound Philargyr hand and foot with chains of gold. After he had thus made him captive, he refused to allow him to return to the upper air, unless he would become his slave, and labour incessantly in bringing new treasures to the mine. It was farther said, that the golden bonds had never from that hour been removed; and that though they were invisible to the naked eye, the signs of their presence might be detected in every look and gesture of the unhappy merchant. Thus his head was continually bent downwards, and his very walk constrained and embarrassed, because the chains and fetters that he wore weighed heavily upon him and impeded his steps.

Strange as this legend seems, it was, in the main, true. One part alone was incorrect. The spirit of the gold mine had not used threats or violence; he had, throughout, accomplished his purpose by treachery, and Philargyr had sunk, imperceptibly, into a state of servitude. His chains had been light and flexible when they were first twined around his limbs. It was while he wore them that, by little and little, they had increased in size and strength. For such was the nature of those bonds, that, when newly wrought, they were most easily broken. For this reason, he was not suffered to feel their pressure until they had been hardened by time; and even then, the change was so gradual, that Philargyr was not aware of it. The signs of his bondage, which seemed so clear to others, passed unnoticed by himself.

Still, however, he was a slave, and by little and little incurred the full misery of servitude, though to the last unconscious of its cause. Morning, noon, and evening, he laboured for an

MEGACLES. Page 35.

insatiable master, who allowed him no share in the profits of his toil. Every day was passed in drudgery and weariness; every night in anxiety and care. Not an hour was given him to share the amusements of his fellow-citizens; not an hour for the duties of hospitality; not an hour for the quiet enjoyment of home. His whole time was claimed by the spirit of the gold mine; and very heavy and monotonous was the task imposed upon him. If a child were forced to go on, hour after hour, casting up a sum the figures of which were innumerable, he might form some idea of the employment of Philargyr. His wealth was to him but as an endless sum, and his most successful enterprises did but add some new figure to the account.

Yet even this would give no just notion of his misery. He could not help believing the old man's warning, though his whole life was at variance with his belief. He knew that his buried treasure would be worse than useless when the day of his exile arrived. The gates of the Glorious City would be closed against him, and endless wanderings in the dreary wilderness were certain to succeed the present season of anxiety and toil. His heart often shrank within him, as he witnessed the averted looks of the Messengers of the Great King. They did not even offer to carry his treasures to the Royal Palace, for long experience had taught them that it was a waste of words to seek employment from Philargyr. Again and again had he resolved to entrust them with some portion of his wealth, but the subtle chains of gold withheld his hand, and, while he was struggling against them, the opportunity passed by, and he deferred till the morrow his intended gift.

While the eldest of the four brothers thus laboured incessantly for the spirit of the mine, the second was following a very different path. He was unfettered by any chain of gold, and his bearing was high and noble; his step firm and free. He looked down on his very riches with disdain, and they won him the envy and admiration of his fellow-citizens instead of their pity and contempt. But while, in every other respect, his conduct afforded a marked contrast to that of Philargyr, there was one important point in which he resembled him. He neglected altogether the old man's warning.

There was a district in Metœcia, far removed from the stir and traffic of the crowded streets, and farther still from the dwellings of the King's Messengers. It was remarkable for the beauty and costliness of its buildings. The erection of these formed a favourite occupation of the more wealthy merchants. Their appearance was very irregular, for the size and form of each varied with the taste and resources of the individual who raised it. But all might be comprehended under two great classes. Some were frail and unsubstantial, and intended to please the eye for one short summer, and then make way for others not less perishable than themselves; while some were built of firm and durable materials, in the hope that they might stand for centuries as memorials of their architects. The one class were for the most part called villas of Pleasure; the other, towers of Fame.

It was to the erection of one of these latter that Megacles devoted his vast wealth. The whole energy of his mind was given to this single object, and its gradual accomplishment was watched by his fellow-citizens with the most eager interest. The raising of the tower formed quite an epoch in the history of Metœcia. Wonderful stories were told of the depth of its foundations and the thickness of its walls. Each of the vast stones seemed to have its own legend annexed to it, while the quarry from which they came, and the names of the workmen, and every detail connected with the building, were carefully preserved in the annals of the city. But all this I must pass over very briefly, for the King's Messengers had no share in the work; and from this cause the whole narrative of the tower, which appeared so eventful to Megacles and his brother merchants, has but little interest in the present story.

The whole soul of Megacles was ab sorbed in the erection of the building; —and these few words comprise his history. He did not keep aloof from his fellow-citizens, but he made his intercourse with them subservient to this one object. If he visited the crowded streets, it was in order to select workmen of skill and strength. If he went into the market-place, it was to change his gold and jewels for blocks of marble and granite. His perseverance was rewarded, and his work prospered. Day after day the tower increased in size and beauty. It was to no purpose that the wind and storm beat against it; the firm foundations defied their power. The wreck of the surrounding buildings was made to assist its growth. Some of these had been left as fragments, in consequence of the sudden exile of their architects. Some were mouldering away with the lapse of time; and some were purposely undermined by the workmen of Megacles. He selected from the ruins of each such stones as seemed suited for the accomplishment of his design; until at length his tower rose so far above every other in the city, that it appeared to stand by itself in solitary grandeur.

The more it grew, the more was the mind of Megacles absorbed in its growth. It seemed to exercise a fascination over him, and from the day in which it became visible from every part of the city, his eye was seldom withdrawn from it. This may in part account for his neglect of the King's Messengers. His look was raised above them while he watched his tower. Even if they ventured to speak to him, their voices failed to arrest his attention; for his ear had been so long filled with the din and tumult of building, that it had been rendered deaf to any gentler sound.

Yet, notwithstanding his success, Megacles was not happy. He was perpetually changing or adding to his tower. It never seemed to have attained the perfection that he designed. He remembered also how the city of Metœcia was liable to the shock of earthquakes, so that at any moment the vast fabric mignt be shaken from its foundation, and reduced to a heap of ruins. Neither was this all. Even at those times in which he was able to view with unmingled satisfaction the tower itself, there was still a cloud upon his vision of glory. It had arisen, in the first instance, from the simple question of a poor wayfaring man. Megacles had observed him gaze earnestly at the building, and then turn aside, as though to conceal his tears. He could not help inquiring what train of thoughts it had called forth, to lead to such an expression of sorrow. There was a strange sadness in the wayfarer's reply. "I was thinking," he said, "how long this vast tower was calculated to last." "How long!" exclaimed Megacles, with indignant pride; "centuries on centuries will elapse, and there shall be no symptoms of decay." "And I was also thinking," he continued, in the same melancholy tone, "how long its possessor will remain within its walls!"

The wayfarer had disappeared before Megacles could reply; but the unwelcome words kept recurring to his mind in spite of every effort to suppress them. It was true that only half the period usually allotted to the merchants for their sojourn in Metœcia had as yet passed by; but he knew that, at any moment, his sentence of exile might be pronounced, and that the strength of his tower would not delay its enforcement for a single hour. The warning of the old man now came back to his remembrance, and brought with it new feelings of disquietude and alarm. Where were the immense riches that had been intrusted to his care? Had any portion of them been laid up in the Royal Palace? Alas! he shrank from the reply. He had not, indeed, buried them in the earth like Philargyr. On the contrary, he had often lavished them with an unsparing hand. But, while he had seldom failed to examine those who came for them on their health, their strength, and their skill in building, he had forgotten the one only important question,—he had never asked, whether they were Messengers of the Great King.

There was a time when, as these thoughts passed through the mind of Megacles, he half formed the resolution of pulling down, stone by stone, the tower which he had raised, and giving the materials to the King's Messengers. But the dread of ridicule and pride of heart prevailed. He felt that he should incur the mockery of his brother merchants, if, after years of incessant labour, his own hand were to destroy the sole produce of his toil. He once more fixed his gaze stedfastly on the lofty building, and resolved to suppress every doubt and alarm. His efforts were at length successful. Not only did his former triumphant feeling return, but a yet more fatal delusion seized him. He fancied the story of the King's Messengers, and the Royal

EUPREPES. Page 47.

Palace, and the Glorious City, to be a mere invention; and maintained that notwithstanding the law of Exile, the only sure and lasting resting-place was to be found in the tower of Fame.

Alas! even while he was giving vent to these boastful words, his own sentence of exile had gone forth, and the bearer of the Royal Mandate was at hand. But we must leave him awhile, to follow the history of the two remaining brothers.

The King's Messengers.

CHAPTER III.

'Tis not the eye of keenest blaze,
  Nor the quick swelling breast,
That soonest thrills at touch of praise:
  These do not please him best.
But voices low and gentle,
  And timid glances shy,
That seem for aid parental
  To sue all wistfully.

CHRISTIAN YEAR

THE story of Euprepes, the third brother, differs greatly from the two that have preceded it. The warning of the old man did not merely leave a transient impression upon his mind, but gave a colouring to his whole course of action. He talked of it loudly and frequently to his fellow-citizens, and described, in affecting language, the wonderful vision which the mirror had disclosed. As soon as he received his share of his father's wealth, he resolved to spend no portion on the pleasures of the city, but to transmit the whole to the King's Palace.

He did not fail to make public his intention; and there was no lack of Messengers. First one, then another came, each with his own tale of poverty or distress, and each promising to carry safely the treasure committed to his trust. Euprepes gave to all alike with an unsparing hand; but he soon grew weary of the monotony of the employment. All went on quietly day after day. There was no interest or excitement. His proceedings were either unobserved or disregarded by the greater part of the inhabitants of the city. He fancied that this was, in part, the fault of his Messengers. As soon as they received his gifts, they used studiously to conceal them and shrink from the observation of those who met them in the streets. In order to prevent this, he directed that they should carry the bags of money openly in their hands, and from time to time give public notice of the object of their journey Some few refused compliance, and were immediately dismissed his service.

This expedient, in part, succeeded. The Messengers were often seen and questioned, and more than one friend congratulated Euprepes on the store he was laying up in the Royal Palace. Still, however, he was dissatisfied. He required something more than this. The way of sending the money seemed to him out of keeping, both with the vastness of his wealth and with the important object for which it was sent. Bright visions would cross his mind of long triumphal processions through the streets of the city, and of shouts and acclamations attending their progress.

Now, while he was indulging these thoughts, a man in the garb of a herald stood before him. His form, at first, was dim and uncertain; but as the young merchant gazed upon it, it gradually increased in distinctness. He wore a gorgeous livery, and had a golden trumpet in his hand. He thus addressed himself to Euprepes:—"Your noble purpose has been long known to me; neither have you been remiss in carrying it into effect. But there is one thing which you have forgotten. Such wealth as yours should not be trusted to a few scattered Messengers, who wander, some here and some there, and hide themselves in the obscure corners of the city. You require the assistance of a herald to summon them all at a stated period, and then to marshall them in their ranks, and arrange the order of their procession, Let, then, that office be mine."

The whole complexion of the life of Euprepes was changed by this proposal. He at once adopted the herald's suggestion, and the monotony of which he had complained passed away. From henceforth his embassies to the Royal Palace excited no less interest in the city than the tower of Megacles, while they proved to himself a source of perpetual triumph. It will be sufficient to describe one of them; for, though they seemed to his brother merchants to pre sent an endless variety of appearance, the principal features in all are in reality alike, and the first embassy that he sent will give a true view of his history.

When the day for the grand procession had been fixed, the herald sounded his trumpet, and proclaimed it far and wide through the streets of the city. In the meanwhile the young merchant collected many costly bales of merchandise, and exchanged a large quantity of jewels for silver and gold. As all this was done publicly in the market-place, it tended greatly to increase the general interest. The doors of his own mansion were closed, and the few solitary Messengers who came to them, from time to time, were dismissed with orders to return together on the day announced by the herald.

On the appointed morning the windows of the neighbouring houses were thronged with spectators. Presently the crowd thickened in the street, until the whole of it was blocked up by persons professing to be King's Messengers. So vast was the concourse that many a poor widow and orphan struggled in vain to pass through it, and returned sadly to their own homes without once obtaining a sight of the dwelling of Euprepes. At midday the young merchant appeared. He was attended by a splendid retinue of friends; near him were the bales of goods and the gold and silver which he was about to distribute, but nearer still was the herald, who never failed to keep closely to his side. The sun shone fully upon them; and as its rays were reflected back by their bright apparel and the golden trumpet and the precious metals that lay scattered upon the ground, the air was rent with the acclamations of the assembled multitudes.

After the shouts had continued some minutes, the herald proclaimed silence; and Euprepes, taking coins of various sizes from the heaps at his side, scattered them indiscriminately among the people. A scene of fearful confusion followed, while each Messenger struggled for his share. Many of the most weak and sickly were crushed and trodden under foot. The young merchant could see but a small portion of their sufferings, yet even that gave rise to painful thoughts; but the whisperings from within were quickly suppressed by the loud voice of the herald, as he proclaimed "Hasten, hasten, ye Messengers; gather up the treasures of Euprepes the merchant, which he bids you bear to the distant Palace of the Great King."

It was not until the vast stores which Euprepes had provided for the occasion were exhausted, that the tumult ceased. And then the herald arranged the Mes sengers in a long procession, that they might march publicly through the city. It was a strange sight to see that troop of miserable objects, moving along to the sound of a trumpet, with all the external signs of triumph and joy. The misery of their general appearance formed, for the most part, a singular contrast to the costly burthens which they bore. Many of them seemed conscious of this, and shrank instinctively from the observation of their fellows; but none were permitted to desert the order of march; and ever, as they advanced onward, the voice of the herald proclaimed louder and louder, "Behold, ye citizens, behold the riches of Euprepes, which he sends before him to the distant Palace of the Great King.

The procession was so arranged as to be kept continually within view of the young merchant. He watched its course through the market-place, and up and down the principal streets of the city.

From the point at which he stood he could hear distinctly the shouts of the populace and the proclamation of the herald; and there he remained, watching and listening, until the shades of evening closed in, and the reality was lost in a bright and beautiful dream. For in the visions of the night procession after procession continued to pass before him; they were all laden with costly offerings for the Royal Palace,—some of silver and gold, some of bales of merchandise, some of glorious apparel,—but they kept moving round and round the city, and with the inconsistency of a dream it did not seem strange to Euprepes that, though bound on a distant journey, they never passed beyond its walls.

Such was the general aspect of the

processions of Euprepes. Some exceeded others in pomp and magnificence; but each was proclaimed by the same trumpet, and set in order by the same herald; so that, as I before said, one description will suffice for them all.

Meanwhile, his resources seemed inexhaustible. It was as though his treasure kept returning to himself, and the more he gave the more he had to bestow. Of all the brothers he was by far the most popular; his sojourn in the city was cheered alike by the praises of the rich and the blessings of the poor. There were, indeed, some who murmured and repined, but their complaints were drowned by the trumpet of the herald, and never reached the ears of Euprepes. He believed himself to be idolized by all within the city, at the same time that he was laying up for himself an inexhaustible store of wealth beyond its walls. Sometimes his feelings were those of quiet self-complacency, sometimes of joyous triumph; but they were rarely overclouded by the slightest shadow of doubtfulness or alarm. The pursuits of his elder brothers were regarded by him with a kind of contemptuous compassion. He would often stand in the bright sunshine on the rising ground where his house was built, and point in derision to the tower of Megacles, or describe with bitterness the yet sadder slavery of Philargyr; and then following with his eye the long train of his own Messengers, he would conclude by saying, "I, too, have my tower, but it

PHILARGYR. Page 61.

is built on a surer foundation; I, too, have my treasures, but I have sent them to a safer home!"

The story of the fourth brother I cannot tell, for but little is known of his history. He did not resemble either Philargyr or Megacles, for he neither toiled and laboured for the spirit of the gold mine, nor built for himself a tower of fame; and yet he was also unlike Euprepes, for no herald attended him on his walks, and there was no array of Messengers to be seen continually at his door. Much of his time was passed in seclusion. His occupations were unknown; and he sojourned in the city of Metœcia as one who scarcely belonged to it. Those who watched with the greatest interest the different pursuits of the three elder brothers, were gradually led to forget the very existence of Sophron. There was no great event to mark it or force it upon their attention. At one time, indeed, he did excite a momentary sensation. He left the quarter of the city inhabited by the wealthy merchants, and made choice of a more lowly mansion, surrounded by the dwellings of the poor. His motives even for this change were never discovered. Some ascribed it to avarice, some to want. But it soon ceased to be a topic of conversation; and he was consigned to greater obscurity than before.

To the few friends who continued to visit him in his retirement, he was always kind and hospitable; but there was a mystery about his way of life which they were unable to penetrate. As time went on, he still seemed to grow poorer and poorer. Some secret drain appeared to exhaust his wealth. No sign of luxury was seen in his abode; his dress was changed for one of less costly materials; and his diet was of the simplest kind. All this was of itself strange, but there was something yet more unaccountable in the effect that it had upon Sophron himself. Every day his step grew lighter, and his countenance more full of joy. The look of depression and anxiety which during the days of his abundance he had at times worn, was now never seen upon his brow. One would have ima gined that it was not his wealth, but some heavy burthen that had been taken away from him,—he became so light and cheerful under its removal. When questioned as to the cause of this, he would sometimes answer by a smile, sometimes by a tear; and there were those who said that, though the smile of Sophron never failed to make the heart rejoice, his tear was yet more full of gladness than his smile.

The young merchant was really poor. The cause of his poverty, like the rest of his history, was buried in obscurity; but, whatever became of his money, it did not, like that of Euprepes, keep returning to him again. The praise of men never gilded his deeds of self-sacrifice, neither did earthly glory shed its brightness upon his path. And yet, after all, his lowly dwelling was not without its beautiful legend. There were some who could tell how, in the dim twilight, or in the still hour of night, they had seen the train of Royal Messengers moving stealthily from his door. They were not arranged in ranks, like those sent by Euprepes. Every individual walked alone. And yet it was clear that all formed part of the same long procession, for each had his left hand muffled closely in his garments, while with the right he pointed to the East to mark the direction of his journey. Slowly and silently, one by one, they moved onward through the least frequented streets of the city. Not a footfall was heard as they passed along. At length they reached the Eastern gate. It was closed against them, but, like a long line of shadows, the procession still continued its unswerving course, and, passing straight through the opposing barrier, were lost in the darkness beyond.

These things were not, indeed, reported publicly in the city. Few of the wealthy merchants had heard them at all, and fewer still believed them. Those who witnessed them felt their voices hushed by the solemnity of the scene. Its silence seemed, as it were, to rest upon them; and they could only whisper of it from ear to ear, or meditate upon it quietly in their own homes. And when they asked themselves with a thrill of eager interest, whither that long procession had gone, a voice within them would reply, "It is gone far, far beyond the boundaries of the city,—the barriers were unable to arrest its progress,—and it now bears the treasures of Sophron to the distant Palace of the Great King."

Such was the legend; but there is one part of it which yet remains to be told. It was said that when the few, who had witnessed the secret procession, returned to the street in which the merchant lived, they perceived his doorway to be strewed with pearls, while an amber light shone around his dwelling, and strains of gentle music were heard from within its walls. So soft was that light, that it seemed but to shed its colouring on the surrounding darkness—so quiet that music, that the stillness of the night was unbroken by the sound. They stood gazing at a distance. They were afraid to venture near, lest, like a scene of enchantment, it should vanish from their view; and there was a fascination in it, which would not suffer them to depart. The eye never grew weary of watching that lovely radiance, nor the ear of listening to that celestial melody. At length the sun arose, and then the vision passed away; or rather, though the soft light and quiet music never ceased to bless the house of Sophron, they could not be seen and heard in the glare and turmoil of the day. The pearls also were no longer visible. There were some, indeed, who fancied they could still perceive them; but, when they stooped to gather them, they found only the drops of morning dew which lay upon the ground.

The King's Messengers.

CHAPTER IV.

> We barter life for pottage; sell true bliss
>   For wealth or power, for pleasure or renown;
> Thus, Esau-like, our Father's blessing miss,
>   Then wash with fruitless tears our faded crown.
>
> CHRISTIAN YEAR.

DAYS, months, and years rolled on in the same unvaried course. Philargyr continued to toil and labour, and every hour gathered in fresh riches for his insatiable master. Megacles received early the sentence of Exile, but his tower remained as his memorial in the city. Euprepes still dazzled the eyes of the multitude by his costly gifts and gorgeous processions. Sophron alone lived a life of obscurity. The wealth, the fame, and the liberality of the three elder brothers, had severally passed into a proverb. Many were the discussions concerning their conduct and character; for in spite of the contempt in which Philargyr was generally held, even he had his tribe of flatterers and partisans, and it was remarked that their number increased as the time of his banishment drew near. But no allusion was made to the law of Exile in any of the conversations concerning the brothers. I have already accounted for this silence. Notwithstanding the King's warnings, the citizens, for the most part, were accustomed to regard Metœcia as their lasting dwelling-place. It seemed as though some heavy mist were resting upon them; and their low range of thought was bounded by the narrow circuit of their own walls.

A protracted sojourn in the city fell to the portion of Philargyr, though the progress of time served only to increase the burthen of his servitude. He was carrying a heavy load of gold to the secret mine, and toiling and groaning beneath its weight, when the old man met him on his way. For a moment, he gazed stedfastly on the weary merchant, and then with a smile of bitter irony offered to relieve him. Philargyr trembled. He endeavoured at first to persuade himself that it was but a re-appearance of the same image which he had seen in the mirror; but his limbs tottered, and his cheek grew pale, and there was a numbness at his heart, which convinced him that the actual form of the old man now stood before him, and he could not doubt the nature of the message which he bore.

At length, in much terror and perplexity, and scarcely conscious of the meaning of his own words, he thus addressed him:—"Stranger," he cried, "if, indeed, thou art charged with the sentence of Exile, leave me yet a little while. I have great treasure in this city. Wait till my camels and asses are laden, and my slaves with their bags of gold are ready to accompany us, and then we will hasten on our journey."

But the stranger replied, and the cold, stern accents fell as ice on the heart of Philargyr,—"Oh, merchant, what vain words are these! You know well that whoever travels with me travels alone. Your camels and asses, your slaves, your silver, and your gold cannot accompany us. The wealth that you have sent beforehand to the Royal Palace is now your own; but all that remains in the city is lost to you for ever."

Then did the vision in the mirror rise in distinct and fearful remembrance to the mind of Philargyr. It was but mockery to speak to him of treasure sent beforehand to the Royal Palace. The accumulated gains of his many years of labour were all stored up in the fatal mine. He had counted them over but yesterday; not a single coin was missing—all were there. Now as he thought of this, he turned his eyes imploringly to the old man; but in a moment he again averted his gaze, for he perceived him to be no longer alone. A dark and terrible crowd of attendants were ranged around. They were armed with scourges of iron, which they raised on high, as though ready at any moment to drive him forth into the dreary wilderness that lay beyond the city.

At length, he cried out in accents of mingled fear and remorse, "Alas! O stranger, hitherto I have neglected your warning. The whole of my wealth is still within the city. But, surely, you yourself are a King's Messenger! Have compassion, then, upon me, and even now bear it quickly to the Royal Palace."

But the old man replied, "You ask

what cannot be. I am indeed a King's Messenger, but I bear no treasure with me to the Royal Palace; for all things change at my touch, and crumble into decay. Those charged with that office have been with you long ago,—the poor, the afflicted, and the infirm;—they would have conveyed your riches thither, if you had not driven them empty-handed from your door." Darker and more terrible grew the train of the old man's followers, as Philargyr listened to these fearful words. Once more the iron scourges were raised on high; but the unhappy merchant, in a voice of the deepest misery, implored the respite of a single day.

"To-morrow," he said, "to-morrow, all shall be in readiness. I will even now summon the King's Messengers, and send the whole of my wealth beyond the walls of the city. Spare me, if it be but for a few hours. Your coming was unlooked for, and therefore it has found me unprepared."

"It is false," replied the old man, sternly. "My coming has been very slow and gradual. During the still hours of the night, you heard, one by one, the sound of my footsteps, while I was yet at a distance from the city. Your limbs grew feeble, and your hair grey, and your heart dull and cold; and you knew well that these signs preceded the approach of the last Messenger of the Great King. Each warning made you struggle, for a little while, to separate yourself from your gold. But it held you in bonds; and you could not set yourself free. If I were to leave you now, the result would be the same. You would go on clinging to your riches, or rather they would go on clinging to you, even if you were suffered to remain whole centuries in the city."

Philargyr felt that the old man's words were but too fearfully true. He had for many years been expecting the bearer of the Royal Mandate. So slow had been his approach, that days, weeks, and months, seemed to mark the interval of each succeeding step. Time had been thus allowed for the gradual removal of all his wealth. The appointed Messengers had repeatedly called for it; but after a faint effort to give it them, he had sent them away till the morrow. And the cause of this was, as

I have said, the chain of gold which had been twined round his hands by the spirit of the mine. It had been light and fragile once, but it was a magic chain, which grew more firm and massive with the lapse of years. The time had been, when the captive, by one vigorous struggle, might have set himself free. But each weak and unsuccessful effort served only to increase its strength; and the links had become so firmly riveted, that his own hand was all too feeble to dissolve them now.

The unhappy merchant had, as we have seen, long bent beneath the weight of this chain; but he now perceived it for the first time, as it was wrenched asunder by the iron grasp of the stranger's hand; and in a moment, he was parted for ever from his vast wealth, and, while the scourges fell heavily upon him, driven forth as an exile beyond the walls of the city.

We will now leave Philargyr, and bring to a close the story of Megacles. A no less sad and fearful picture awaits us there. He was, as I have said, summoned early, and the day of his exile followed close on the warning of the wayfaring man. But I have thought it better to make no change in the order of his history.

The old man found him in all the fulness of his strength. He was arrayed in purple and costly apparel, and stood gazing with an eye of pride on the tower which he had raised. A crowd of eager partisans were gathered around. The bearer of the Royal Mandate passed through the midst of them, with a slow and silent step; and his finger had long pointed to Megacles, before he himself became aware of his approach. It was the looks of those who stood around, which first warned him that the day of his exile had arrived.

No sooner, however, did he become conscious of the old man's presence, than he endeavoured to face him with an undaunted air. "Stranger," he said boldly, "your summons to me is vain. I ask no dwelling-place in the Glorious City. Here, in Metœcia, have I built myself a tower; and here, in Metœcia, shall be my lasting home." There was a shout of applause from the surrounding multitude; but the old man neither spoke nor moved. Coldly and stedfastly he gazed upon the merchant, until the proud spirit of Megacles quailed beneath his look, and the boastful words seemed to wither on his lips, while every limb was shaken with convulsive terror. He turned away his face from the unwelcome Messenger, and endeavoured to gather new courage from the contemplation of his tower of Fame. But there was a haze which now encircled it; it appeared to be already fading in the distance; and he could hardly distinguish the building itself from its long dark shadow which rested upon the ground.

At length, the old man broke the silence:—"It is ever thus, O merchant! the objects in this city become, for the most part, the same with their shadows, when I approach them. But take my glass, and you will once more behold distinctly the building that you have raised." As he said this, he held out a glass to Megacles. The merchant took it, almost unconsciously. For a moment he looked through it, and then, with a cold shudder, suffered it to fall from his hand. His lofty tower had dwindled into a sepulchre, when seen through the glass which the stranger had given him. But diminutive as it now appeared, there was an inscription engraved distinctly upon it; and he had read only too plainly these fatal words:—"Here lie the garments which Megacles once wore."

"Yes," said the old man, with a smile of scorn, "it is not for yourself that you have raised this lofty tower, but for the garments which you wear! They shall remain in the city, and rest beneath it, until the moth and worm have eaten them away. But for yourself you have prepared no dwelling-place, and you will be driven forth a homeless wanderer in the wilderness."

The last feeling of self-confidence now died away from the heart of Megacles. Instead of the crowd of eager partisans, he saw only the same gloomy attendants, which afterwards appeared to Philargyr. He felt that his tower would avail him nothing; and that, if the gates of the Royal City were closed against him, no hope of safety could remain. The past rose in bitter remembrance before him; and, as he thought over the numerous workmen that he had employed on his building, he tried to recollect some one among the number who might prove to have been a Messenger of the Great King.

The effort, however, was vain; and the secret feeling of his heart belied his words, as he advanced a claim to treasure in the Royal Palace. "Stranger," he said, "I have not altogether neglected the warning which you gave. My riches are not buried in a mine; I have dispersed them far and near, and know not whither they are gone. Some perhaps may have remained within the city, but surely some portion must have escaped beyond its walls. If the King's Messengers came to me they received their share with the rest: I never wilfully drove them away. Oh tell me, then, that there is some treasure prepared for me in the Royal Palace, and that the gates of the Glorious City will not be closed against me for ever."

But the old man pointed to the tower as he replied, "Behold, Megacles, the one only monument of your wealth; it is there, and there alone, that all who received your wages or your gifts deposited their burthens. You yourself never failed to point it out to them as the object of their journey. But neither is this all; the King's Messengers, though you knew them not, did indeed come to you among the rest. They were weak and helpless, and you loaded them with vast blocks of marble and granite, which they were unable to bear. Many sank beneath their burthens, others were crushed and maimed by stones falling from the building. It is true that their groans and lamentations never reached you. They were drowned by the noise and tumult which accompanied the erection of your tower. But the cries of the King's Messengers are carried by each passing wind to the Royal Palace, and are heard and remembered there."

Megacles would fain have replied, but no time was allowed him for further words. The stranger touched him with his icy hand, and in an instant the dark attendants had stripped him of his raiment, and driven him with their scourges from the city. There were few who wept for his sudden departure, for Megacles was not loved; but his admirers and partisans gathered up his purple garments, and deposited them carefully beneath the tower. In a little while the moth and the worm had consumed them there; while the tower itself continued to stand for many ages, —a vain memorial of the spot where they had been laid.

The King's Messengers.

CHAPTER V.

THERE are in this loud, stunning tide
  Of human care and crime,
With whom the melodies abide
  Of th' everlasting chime;
Who carry music in their heart
  Through dusky lane and wrangling mart,
Plying their daily task with busier feet,
  Because their secret souls a holy strain repeat.

CHRISTIAN YEAR.

EUPREPES saw the sentence of exile passed on both his elder brothers, and spoke with much eloquence of the misery of their fate. For himself, he said that he had long since been fully prepared to depart; all his treasures had been sent before him to the Royal Palace; and he was only anxious for the time when they would be restored to him again. Sometimes he would complain to his friends of the long delay of the bearer of the Royal Mandate, and declare that he was even then listening for his footstep, and would advance to welcome him at the first warning of his approach.

The stranger tarried long; but when he did come, the reality proved very different from the anticipations of Euprepes. In spite of himself, he was conscious of a sensation of fear. First a strange darkness seemed to fall on the objects around him. Then doubts and misgivings flitted like shadows across his mind; and the vision of the future, as well as of the past and present, was arrayed in less bright colouring than before. He advanced to meet the old man, but it was with the unsteady step of one walking in a mist; he addressed him in bold words of welcome, but it was with a faltering voice, as though he felt doubtful of the reply.

"At length," he said, "thou hast arrived! But wherefore didst thou tarry so long? Was it that thy journey was delayed by the frequent train of Messengers that met thee on thy way? They were bearing my silver and my gold, my jewels and my merchandise, to the Great Monarch whom thou servest. I have much wealth laid up for me in his Palace. Come, then, let us hasten thither."

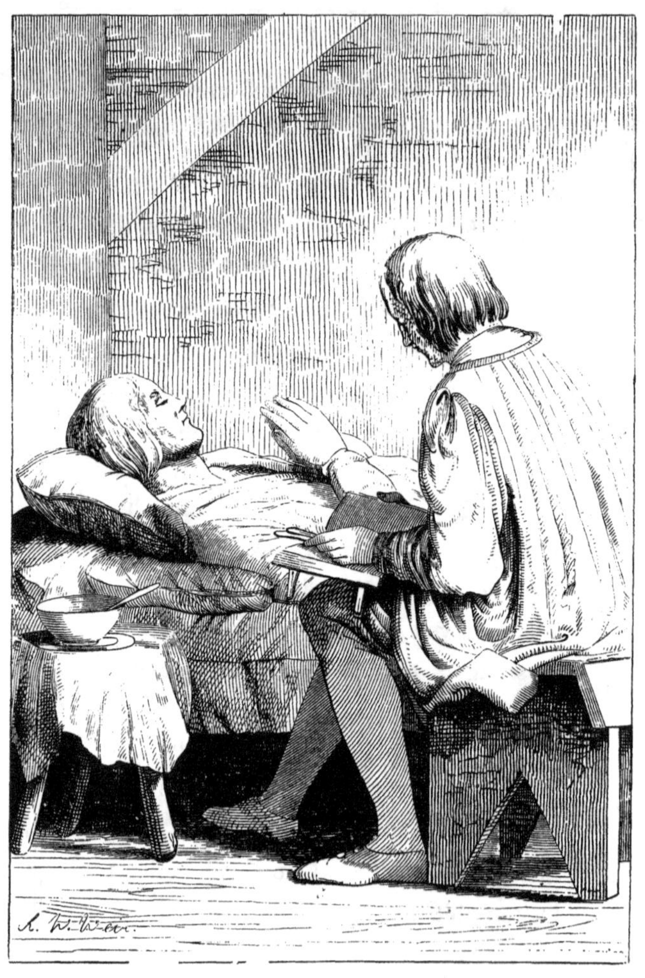

SOPHRON. Page 90.

But the old man offered no reply; he merely fixed his cold, searching gaze upon the merchant; and while he did so, it seemed as though some terrible object rose up between them; and the shadow fell yet more darkly on the mind of Euprepes. He tried in vain to suppress his feelings of anxiety and alarm; they kept following one another like the waves of a troubled sea. At length he was forced to give way to them, and once more spoke to the old man, but with words of less confidence than before. "Stranger," he said, "from whence is this sensation of secret terror! I had looked to your coming as a time of sunshine and joy. Where are the good tidings that you have in store for me? Do not imagine that, like Megacles and Philargyr, I have neglected your warning. My wealth has been distributed among the King's Messengers. Week after week, in long procession, they left my door. Surely, surely, you must have seen many bags of gold and bales of merchandise in the Royal Palace, with the name of Euprepes written upon them!"

The old man replied, or rather, perhaps, though the words seemed to come from him, it was the thoughts of Euprepes which made answer to themselves:—

"Oh merchant! from the city in which you dwell to the land inhabited by the Great King, is a long and dangerous journey. It is true that many a Messenger has of late trodden it in safety, and rich and precious were the burthens which they bore. But a simple cross was the only mark either on the bags of gold or the bales of merchandise. If, therefore, the name of Euprepes was written upon yours, the whole of them must have been lost."

"Lost! lost!" exclaimed the unhappy man, in a voice of agony; "Nay, it cannot be. The embassies were so frequent and numerous that some, at least, must have arrived: and even if it be otherwise, the whole city is a witness that I sent them. The air was rent with acclamations as they passed along; and far and near you could hear the voices of those who cried, 'This is the wealth of Euprepes, which he sends before him to the distant Palace of the Great King.'"

"It is not such sounds as those," replied the old man, "which ever reach the Royal Palace; they are lost in the din and tumult of the city, or heard only by the enemies of the King. But tell me, Euprepes; are you a merchant, and do you not know that those riches are moved most securely which are sent in secrecy and silence? If you had wished merely to transfer your possessions to a house in a neighbouring street, should you, in the first instance, have paraded them before your door, and told the bearers to display them openly to all who met them on their way? Surely, if you had done this, and they had been intercepted by thieves and robbers, the fault would have been your own."

Euprepes could make no reply; and yet he murmured something of a hope that the soldiers of the Great King would not have suffered the Messengers to be plundered on their journey. But the old man, in a sterner voice, thus continued to address him :—

"I will tell you, Euprepes, what has become of your wealth. There is an enchanter that dwells in this city; his name is Pride, and he is an enemy of the Great King. He it was who sent the herald to summon the Messengers to your door. The sound of his trumpet never fails to change the purest gold and silver into brass and glittering tinsel. These were the offerings that you really sent; but even these did not reach the destination for which you intended them. The enchanter wove his magic circles round the feet of your Messengers, so that they followed one another in the same endless track, without ever advancing one step upon their journey."

A new and fearful light now burst upon the mind of Euprepes. He remembered how, in the visions of the night, he had continually seen the long processions moving round and round. Never for a moment had he lost sight of them in the distance, or formed a wish to trace their course beyond the city. Alas! in these dreams he had seen but the image of his actual Messengers, though it was the enchanter who placed before his eyes the glass in which they appeared. His head grew dizzy, and his heart sick, as they rose to his remembrance; but he still made one last effort to lay claim to a recompense from the Great King.

"It was gold," said he,—"it was pure

gold that I gave; and, though it may have been changed and rendered worthless, to me at least it was of real value. If it failed to purchase for me an inheritance in the Royal Palace, it surely ought to have been restored to me again. Philargyr hoarded his vast wealth; Megacles built with his a tower of Fame; mine alone has been unprofitably spent, and brought me no recompense within the city, and yet none beyond its walls."

"Merchant," replied the old man, "You know well that you have long since had your reward. The applause of your fellow-citizens fell like a golden shower upon your path; and their goodwill and gratitude have been to you as bales of costly merchandise. It was thus that the wealth, which you professed to give, never ceased to come back to you again. Like Philargyr, you did but traffic with your possessions, and they brought you in a full and abundant return. Your tower, also, like that of Megacles, is built within the city. It is true that your own hands have not laboured in its erection, but day by day you have stood watching it in secret, and listened to the shouts and acclamations which marked its growth. It may, perhaps, have seemed to you to be rising afar off in the territory of the Great King; but this delusion was caused by the same enchanter who sent you the herald. He spread a mist before your eyes, which made an object appear to be in the distance which was really near at hand. Your range of sight has never passed beyond the boundaries of the city; every hope and wish of your heart has been confined within it, and there also was your treasure and your home."

Then did the attendants with the iron scourges seize upon Euprepes, and strip him of his garments; and he, too, was driven forth into the dreary wilderness. But the scourges were unseen by those who witnessed his departure neither could they hear the fearful words in which the sentence of exile was conveyed. And so it was, that, after he was gone, the long train of his Messengers continued to parade the streets; while the false herald with the golden trumpet proclaimed far and near that the happy exile had been received within the gates of the Glorious City, and that all his treasures had been restored to him there.

Such was the fearful history of the three elder brothers. It is a relief to turn aside from it, and seek a resting-place in Sophron's lowly dwelling. He had wept bitterly for their exile, but he did not, like Euprepes, make a display of his compassion, or boast of his own readiness to depart. His tears had flowed in secret, and his hopes also were cherished in the solitude of his own bosom. Every day he put his little room in readiness for the stranger's coming, and was so constantly preparing for it that he may be almost said to have lived in his immediate presence. Yet he, like the rest, was conscious of some change of feeling when his actual summons arrived.

He was at that time enjoying the quiet beauty of the evening hour. It mattered not that a vase with a few autumnal flowers was the only ornament of his humble abode; and that the flame burnt faint and feebly in the solitary lamp which was standing at their side. Sophron could not really be in darkness, poverty, or alone; for, as the shades of night closed in, the pearls appeared upon his threshold, the soft music spoke to him as a companion, and the amber light shed its radiance around. His heart was full of gratitude for these blessings, when a mingled feeling of awe and sadness stole upon him, and it seemed as though some shadow were moving along the wall. Every object changed as the dark outline fell upon it;—the flame of the solitary lamp burned even more dimly than before, and the autumnal flowers began to wither and decay. It needed not these signs to warn Sophron that it was the same figure that had appeared in the mirror. For a while he watched it with a calm and stedfast gaze; presently a sensation of weariness stole upon him, his thoughts grew confused and indistinct, and at length he sank in a state of partial unconsciousness upon the ground.

When he again opened his eyes, the old man was standing at his side. No gloomy attendants were near, but he held a mirror in his hand. Beneath it were the words—"This is the image of the Past." The scene which it reflected was one that had been long familiar to Sophron, and he did not shrink from beholding it now. From time to time soft shadowy forms moved across the glass; they were, doubtless, the images of the King's Messengers; but the eye of Sophron did not for a moment rest upon them, for ever as they appeared, his thoughts wandered to the Royal Palace and Glorious City.

At length the old man addressed him. "Oh! merchant," he said, "how is this? All signs of wealth and luxury are wont to vanish at my presence, but it is not so with thy abode. Even as I crossed the threshold of thy door, pearls of inestimable value were scattered upon the ground. They can be no part of the treasure of this city; for, when I trod silently upon them, they were not sullied by my step, but only shone with a purer brightness an before!"

"Stranger," replied Sophron, "I

cannot tell. You say truly that they are no part of the treasure of the city The whole of my father's vast wealth could not have purchased one of them. They are as the pearls of the far East, and I have looked upon them as gifts from the Great King; but I know not what hand has scattered them thus plenteously at the threshold of my door."

He had hardly finished speaking, when a shadowy form moved across the mirror, and there was a voice from thence which said, "I was a widow, poor and destitute, but a Messenger of the Great King. I went to Philargyr for relief, and he told me that his money was his own. I came to Sophron, and he spoke soft words of comfort, and ministered to my wants, and bade me take freely of his treasures, for it was for my sake that the Great King had placed them in his hands. I wept with joy and gratitude when I left him; and each tear has been changed by the Great King into a pearl, and remained to this hour on the threshold of his abode."

And the old man said, "Oh! merchant, from whence is this wonderful melody that I hear? Sure I am that none of the musicians in this city could produce such strains. Their harps lose their tunefulness, and their sweetest notes become harsh and discordant when I am standing near. But this music has some magic power. My presence only renders it more distinct and perfect than before, and even my own voice is moved into harmony by the sound."

"Stranger," replied Sophron, "I cannot tell. You say truly that the music has a magic power, for it lends its own tunefulness to all around. To me it has long since breathed a spirit of harmony over the din and discord of this crowded city; every care and anxiety has been changed and modulated by its soothing influence; and the events of day after day have seemed to flow on in perpetual melody. But though the music has thus dwelt in my own home, and I have loved it, and listened to it with gladness, I believe it to be but the echo of a yet sweeter strain which is played afar off in some distant land."

Again there was a voice from the mirror; its accents were low and tremulous, like those of a little child, and it said, "I was an orphan, weak and friendless, but a Messenger of the Great King. I went to Megacles for succour, and he pointed to a block of marble, and bade me raise it on high: but my hands were too feeble for the task; and then his attendants drove me away, and said there was no place for little children in the tower of Fame. I came to Sophron; and he fed me and clothed me, and told me that the house in which he lived had been lent to him as a shelter for the orphan child. Every morning and evening I went in secret to the Great King, and carried with me each precious gift that I received from Sophron; and he bade me take back to him in return the offering of a simple heart overflowing with gratitude and love. So it was that my looks and words became to his home as a perpetual song; and this is the soft music which you hear within its walls."

And the old man said, "Tell me, Sophron, from whence is this light that sheds its radiance on all around? Sure I am that it belongs not to this city; for night has thrown her dark mantle over its streets, and, even if it were otherwise, mists and chilling darkness are the signs of my approach. The flame of your own lamp grew more faint and feeble when my shadow first fell upon it, and is fast expiring now. Whence, then, is it that in thy dwelling there seems to be perpetual day?"

A soft slumber was stealing upon Sophron; his eyes were already closed; his voice was indistinct, and yet it sounded like happy music as for the last time he replied, "Stranger, I cannot tell. The light has indeed shone upon me; nay, is shining upon me now. My eyes are closed, and I see it not; but it is as the sunshine of the heart, and I feel it to be here. Whether it be a reality or a beautiful dream, I am conscious of its presence, though I know not from whence it comes."

Then, for the third time, a voice proceeded from the mirror, as a shadowy form moved across it, and it said, "I had been rich and prosperous, but a long sickness brought me into poverty and distress. I heard the proclamation of Euprepes, and made a feeble effort to reach his door; but the crowd, and the glare, and the noise of the trumpet overwhelmed me with fear and shame. I shrank back in silence, and hid myself in the obscurity of my own solitary dwelling. Sophron sought me out and found me there. He tended me in my sickness and ministered to my wants, and bade me be of good cheer, for I had a secret store of wealth, even the prayers and blessings of a poor man; and, when I spoke to him of gratitude, he asked me to give him some portion of my treasure. Then did I remember that poverty and distress had made me a Messenger of the Great King, and I hastened to the Royal Palace, and took with me thither my blessings and my prayers. The Great King received them from me, and shed them as rays of unchanging sunshine on the abode of Sophron, and from thence comes the amber light that yet lives within its walls."

There was a pause of a few seconds; while Sophron appeared to be yielding more and more to the soothing influence of sleep. And then the old man breathed softly upon him, and said, "Thrice happy merchant! Well, indeed, hast thou traded with thy wealth! Thou hast bartered thy perishable silver and gold for the widow's gratitude, the orphan's love, and the poor man's prayer. Now that thou art going hence, these riches will follow thee. The costly pearls, the gentle music, and the amber light shall attend thee on thy journey even to the gates of the Glorious City. But a more abundant treasure, a more perfect harmony, and a light of brilliance unutterable, await thee there."

As he thus spoke, he placed a second

mirror before the eyes of Sophron; and though they now seemed to be sealed in slumber, a smile of joy and gladness played across his countenance. I cannot tell how bright and glorious was the vision that he saw. This alone I know, that the image of the Future was reflected in that glass, and that, as the old man held it, his own form faded away. For a moment there was a sound as of the rustling of many wings in the air, and then all was stillness in the dwelling of Sophron.

On the morrow, the sun shone brightly upon the city;—there was the usual hum of traffic and moving to and fro of the busy multitude in the streets, though the lamp had been extinguished in Sophron's abode, and the aged merchant was gone. Very few of the passers-by noticed the deserted dwelling; but the King's Messengers wept as they beheld it from a distance, and there was a strain of sadness in the gentle music of the orphan child. They mourned, because their own office was at an end; but when they thought of Sophron, their sorrow was turned into joy. They knew that his treasures had been marked with the Cross, and were stored up for him in the Royal Palace, and that he himself was dwelling in the happy city where the law of Exile was unknown.

Conclusion.

A SILENCE of some minutes succeeded the story. Both the children were grave and thoughtful. Leonard looked anxious to say something, but seemed to want courage to begin the conversation. To relieve him from his embarrassment, Mr. Mertoun addressed himself in the first instance to Mary.

"Tell me, Mary," he said, "do you suppose there ever was a city with the same singular law as that of Metœcia?"

"O yes, uncle," she replied readily, "I guessed at once what you intended by it: the story is an allegory, and the law of Exile is the law of Death."

"It is so," said Mr. Mertoun. "The whole world is but our city of Metœcia. We are liable, at any moment, to be called upon to depart from it; and, when our summons comes, we go forth alone, and no part of our possessions follow us. If we live in forgetfulness of this law, our conduct is, to say the least, as unaccountable as that of the merchants in the story. But what do you understand by the vision in the mirror?"

Mary hesitated, and Leonard answered for her, "I suppose, uncle, the thoughts awakened by the death of friends."

"You are right," said Mr. Mertoun; "our seasons of bereavement are those in which we feel most distinctly the nothingness of worldly treasures, and are led to take a true view of our position as pilgrims and sojourners upon earth. The warnings of Holy Scripture, which we may have often heard and disregarded, are then so forced upon our minds, that we cannot set them aside. But tell me, Leonard, what particular duty connected with the instability of riches is the story designed to illustrate?"

The boy coloured as he replied, "The duty of giving to the poor;—and I know why you told it us. But," he added, with some slight hesitation, "I hope you do not think that I am like Philargyr?"

"I have seen but little of either you or Mary," answered Mr. Mertoun, "and cannot even tell to which of the three dangerous paths pointed out in the allegory your natural dispositions may incline. But my design in telling it was to bring distinctly before you the important office assigned to the poor in the Gospel. I was afraid that you were unmindful of it when a few days since you used the words, 'Only some poor man.'"

"I was, indeed," he answered; "and for the future, I will try to look upon the poor as Messengers of the Great King. But, uncle," he continued, after a pause, "do you mean that all who neglect almsgiving are like some one or other of the merchants in the story?"

"I think," replied Mr. Mertoun, "that all, who abuse their riches, may be comprehended under the three great classes that I have described. First, we have those like Philargyr, who do not spend them at all: next, those like Megacles, who spend them, but not on proper objects: and, lastly, those like Euprepes, who spend them, and on proper objects, but not with a proper motive."

"It was not quite that which I intended to ask," said Leonard. "Is it not possible to be partly like one and partly like another?"

"Undoubtedly," replied Mr. Mertoun; "I have, in the story, purposely kept the lines clear and distinct, in order to trace the course of each separately. But in actual life they often seem to cross one another, and without careful self-examinatior we cannot tell to which path even we ourselves may be inclining. There is, however, a yet more important difference between actual life and the allegory. The merchants are represented only as the possessors of great wealth, and with the single duty of almsgiving. Is that a complete view of our position as Christians?"

"Oh no," replied Mary; "you said, when you explained to us the Parable of the Talents, that our health, our time, our affections, and the events of our daily life, all form part of the Talents for which we shall have to account."

"They do," said Mr. Mertoun; "and the Talent of Wealth, though distinct from the rest, never in actual life stands apart from them. The exercise of it must be kept in harmony with the discharge of our other duties. The amount and manner of our alms should depend, not merely on our means, but on the circumstances in which we are placed. It may be laid down as a general rule, that the wish to give, and to give without ostentation, should be a moving principle with all alike; but in each particular instance it will be controlled and limited by a variety of events that it is impossible to define. There is yet another omission in the allegory."

"Do you mean," asked Leonard, "that the merchants only received a single warning, and went on in the same course to the end of their career?"

"It was not that to which I referred," answered Mr. Mertoun, "though certainly, in that respect also, their supposed case is but an imperfect representation of our own. Each line in the story is brought almost uninterruptedly to an end. In actual life, they may be broken off by God's mercy, and Philargyr, or Megacles, become as Sophron. Still, however, the allegory is a true representation of the course of unrepented sin. The omission of which I speak occurs rather in the history of the youngest brother."

"You mean," said Mary, "that we cannot really lay up for ourselves riches in heaven, and that all we do is accepted for the sake of our Saviour. But was not that intended by the mark of the cross which was seen on the merchandise?"

"It is implied in it," replied Mr. Mertoun, "but it does not form, so to speak, any distinct feature in the allegory."

"But ought there to be so many omissions in the story?" asked Mary.

Mr. Mertoun replied, by taking up a drawing which happened to be lying on the table: "Tell me," he said, "do you know of what this is a picture?"

"Of the church," she replied, in some surprise at the question.

"Indeed!" said her uncle. "But I do not see the east window, or the north transept, and but very little of the west end of the building. It seems to me, that three sides of the church are wanting."

"Of course," answered Mary, as she partly guessed his meaning, "it must be so, for the view is taken from the south."

"So, Mary," said Mr. Mertoun, "the view of life in the story is necessarily taken from one particular point. It looks upon it as it were, towards the side of wealth. There are other sides no less important to the symmetry of the building, but they cannot all be introduced into the same picture. I have yet another question to ask:—Do you suppose that the person who sketched this drawing, drew a plan of the foundation of the church before he began it?"

"Nay," replied Mary, "you cannot be serious in asking."

"Well, then," continued Mr. Mer

toun, "in this respect also it is an imperfect picture. The real walls undoubtedly have a foundation, and the building could not stand an instant if it were not there. Do you see my meaning, Leonard?"

"I do," he answered; "you mean, that the death of our SAVIOUR is the foundation on which the walls of our actual life rest; and that, though it be not represented in the story, it is, of course, assumed to be there."

"Exactly so," said Mr. Mertoun, "And I wish you to mark clearly the distinction between this illustration and the former. The several duties of life are like the different walls of the building, which may be brought out in greater or less distinctness, according to the point from which we view it. The doctrine of the atonement is to the Christian as the one foundation on which they rest, and without it the picture could not be really faithful, for the building itself would cease to exist. But to return to the duty of almsgiving. Can you tell me any passage in Holy Scripture in which it is insisted upon to the apparent exclusion of others? You were mentioning, Mary, the Parable of the Talents. Do you remember the description of the Day of Judgment, which follows it?" *

Mary reflected a moment, and then answered, "Those on the King's right hand were rewarded, because they had fed the hungry, given drink to the thirsty, and received the stranger."

* St. Matt. xxv. 34, 35.

"They were so," said Mr. Mertoun; "and our Blessed LORD assured them, that inasmuch as they had done this unto one of the least of His brethren, they had done it unto Himself. In like manner, those on the King's left hand are represented as being punished simply for neglect of the poor. There are also two parables concerning rich men, in which the same view is brought no less distinctly before us."

"One of them," said Leonard, "is that of the Rich Man and Lazarus."*

"It is so," answered his uncle; "no other sin of the rich man is there pointed out to us but that of neglecting the poor beggar who lay at his door. The other parable to which I referred is that of the Rich Man, who, when his

* St. Luke xvi. 19–31.

ground brought forth plentifully, determined to hoard the produce.* GOD punished him with the immediate sentence of death. And our SAVIOUR himself has annexed to it the warning, 'So is he that layeth up treasure for himself, and is not rich towards GOD.'"

"Children," observed Leonard, "are never very rich."

The words were spoken in a low tone, as though in answer to his own thoughts. His uncle, however, did not let them pass unnoticed. "They are not," he replied, "according to the ordinary meaning of the word wealth. But recollect how the mite of the poor widow was pronounced by our Blessed LORD to be more than all the costly gifts which were cast into the treasury by the rich.

* St. Luke xii. 16–21

Now the youngest child may either give a like offering to that of the widow, or he may hoard it up, or spend it on himself."

"And if he does hoard it up," asked Leonard, "will he be like Philargyr?"

"Not, I trust," answered Mr. Mertoun, "such as he was in the end of his career. But his bonds were, at first, light and flexible; it was time that added to them their weight and strength; and such bonds are often worn in secret by children. They are by no means free from the temptation to avarice. The apparently slight opportunities they have for its indulgence render it less perceptible, but not less dangerous. There is no need of a gold mine to foster it. The first trifling coin a child receives is often formed into the first link of the chain that binds him in after-years. If it be followed by the love of money for its own sake, and the wish for more, he is already beginning to share the servitude of Philargyr."

The children were silent. The words awakened no painful thoughts in Mary, for avarice was not one of her failings. But Leonard felt the full force of this application of the story. The gift which he had received from his uncle the preceding Christmas had been hoarded up in secret, and was loved because it was gold. At length he asked in what way the fault of avarice might be cured.

Mr. Mertoun guessed the motive of the question, and replied, "The best remedy for all our faults, my dear boy, is to make them the subject of continual prayer. But this, perhaps, more than any other, requires the resistance of an immediate effort. The conquering it is really like the breaking of a chain. Once summon resolution to give, and it seems as though some spell were dissolved, and the disposition to give more abundantly will follow. I do not mean that the temptation to save will not again come back; but it will return after each defeat with less violence than before, until at length it will be subdued altogether, by the habit of giving. You must not, however, forget that the hoarding up our money is not the only abuse of the talent of wealth; the spending it on improper objects is one no less dangerous; and I believe that children, in general, are more frequently tempted to follow the path of Megacles than that of Philargyr."

"Of Megacles, uncle!" said Mary, in some surprise; "I had fancied that his sin was ambition, and not extravagance."

"It was so," said Mr. Mertoun; "but he may be taken as representing a yet larger class. His history brings especially before us the folly of wasting on some mere earthly object those riches which might be laid up in the treasury of Heaven. To do this is, in reality, extravagance. It matters not, to use the language of the story, whether we build with them mere villas of Pleasure or towers of Fame. Children, who spend what they have on self-gratification to the neglect of the poor, are beginning to follow the course of Megacles."

"But can they be also like him in his ambition?" asked Mary.

"Undoubtedly," answered her uncle, "but the ways in which they can purchase this species of self-gratification are so apparently trivial, that you may have some difficulty in tracing the resemblance. Perhaps the spending money on finery or anything else intended to excite the admiration of their companions, is their nearest approach to the particular sin of Megacles. But is it not said at the conclusion of the story, that Euprepes, also, had in secret been raising a tower?"

"It is," answered Mary; "and it means, that while professing to relieve the poor, he was, like Megacles, merely seeking the applause of his fellow-citizens."

"This, then," continued Mr. Mertoun, "is a kind of ambition to which children are peculiarly exposed. There is no way in which they can purchase applause so readily as by giving to the poor. Each act of benevolence is sure to be accompanied by a certain amount of praise. And yet if they make that the prevailing motive for their gift, they have their recompense upon earth, and will forfeit it in Heaven. Do you remember the warning which our SAVIOUR gave His disciples on this subject?"

"He told them," answered Mary, "that if they did their alms before men, to be seen of them, they would have no reward of their Father in Heaven."

"Yes," continued Mr. Mertoun, "and He added the precept—'When thou doest alms, let not thy left hand know what thy right hand doeth: that thine alms may be in secret: and thy Father Which seeth in secret, Himself shall reward thee openly.'* Is there any difficulty suggested to you by these words?"

"I was wishing to ask," said Leonard, "whether they mean that we are to make a secret of every thing that we give."

"They cannot mean that," answered Mr. Mertoun, "for our LORD has also told us to let our light so shine before men, that they may see our good works, and glorify our Father Which is in Heaven.† By the command, 'not to let our left hand know what our right hand doeth,' we must understand, that we ought to shrink even from any feeling of self-satisfaction at

* St. Matt. vi. 3, 4. † Ibid. v. 16.

our own good deeds, and, of course, yet more to avoid the applause of the world. But we cannot help actually knowing what we ourselves give, and at times it is our duty to let others know it also."

"And yet," observed Mary, "if we do this, are we not really giving our alms before men?"

"Yes," replied Mr. Mertoun, "but not necessarily in order to be seen of them. It is the giving with this object that is forbidden by our Blessed Lord. Almsgiving is no easy duty, and children especially require the advice of others in the manner of its performance. They cannot even find out for themselves proper objects of benevolence. They may, therefore, ask to be taught how to give, and place their offerings in the hands of their friends, and yet look for no other recompense than that which is promised to them in Heaven. Do you remember, Mary, how, when you were a little child, your mother would come to hear you say your prayers, and yet you did not say them in order to be heard of her: she taught you to pray, but the words were addressed to God. Do you understand me?"

"I think so," she replied; "but will there be no difference at all between children who give merely that their friends may praise them and those who give from right motives?"

"Perhaps, at times, there may be no visible difference," answered Mr. Mertoun, "but there must always be a real one. Recollect, that when it is said, 'Which seeth in secret,' it does not mean only that God sees into the secret chamber, but into the secret thoughts of the heart. He can read clearly and distinctly the exact motive of every gift; and as those which profess to be studiously concealed, may in their very concealment proceed from ostentation, so also those which are openly given, may, in His sight, be as the silent offerings of Sophron."

But Mary was not yet quite satisfied. "I know, uncle," she said, "that we must try to be like Sophron in the motive of our alms; but cannot children be in any way like him in the manner of giving them?"

"Yes," answered Mr. Mertoun, "they may be like him in this also, though the resemblance is an imperfect one. They may avoid all unnecessary display; or again, they may conceal what they have already given, or the inward struggle by which the gift is accompanied, or the self-denial which it costs them. All this is as a secret store, which adds to the value of our offerings in the sight of God, if we look for our recompense to Him alone. But it is difficult to lay down any exact rule. The line which, as I have said, is purposely kept distinct and separate in the story, often seems perplexed and difficult, when we try to trace it through the conflicting circumstances of life. I think, however, that you will seldom find any practical difficulty. While we walk along our appointed path, though we cannot see far into the distance, each separate step is for the most part sufficiently clear. Only keep distinctly in your remembrance that the poor are sent to you by GOD; that it cannot be right to hoard up your money, or spend it on your own gratifications, while you do nothing to relieve their wants; and that your offerings must be made for CHRIST's sake, and without the hope of any earthly recompense; and the story of the King's Messengers will not have been told you in vain. The events of your own daily life will best enable you to apply it to yourselves."

With the exception of a single question, Leonard had been a silent listener to the close of the conversation. He did not seem to participate in the difficulties of his sister. When, however, the usual time came for the children to retire to rest, he appeared anxious to remain behind; but Mary called him, and he accompanied her. Mr. Mertoun was left alone. He had seen that the children were impressed by the story but his joy at this circumstance was checked by the remembrance that in a little while the feelings awakened by it would pass away. His thoughts were interrupted by a light footstep at the door; the handle was softly turned, and Leonard entered, alone. There was something in his hand which glittered, and this he gave his uncle, with a few whispered words. The tear rose to Mr. Mertoun's eyes, as he replied, "God bless you, my dear nephew; you have indeed found out the true moral to my story. Go on as you have begun, and your path will be clear." The offering which the boy gave was the long-hoarded gold, and the whispered words were, "For the Messenger of the Great King, who came this morning to your door.'

OTHER WORKS BY THE AUTHOR OF

The King's Messengers,

PUBLISHED BY THE GEN. PROT. EPISCOPAL S. S. UNION

THE SHADOW OF THE CROSS,
An Allegory.—With beautiful Engravings, from designs by CHAPMAN.

THE DISTANT HILLS,
An Allegory.—Illustrated as above.

THE OLD MAN'S HOME,
With beautiful Engravings, from designs by WEIR.

THE FALL OF CRŒSUS.

LIFE OF BISHOP HEBER.

BY THE REV. J. N. NORTON.

This is one of the author's most interesting histories for the reading of the young. The subject has uncommon interest, and is treated with a genial appreciation.—*Banner of the Cross.*

The Life of Heber is in Mr. Norton's best style. It contains as much information about him as could be compressed into so small a compass, and precisely that information which it was most desirable to present to those whom tender age or want of leisure might prevent from seeking it in large volumes.—*The Monitor.*

This little biography will be of peculiar use to those who have not the means of obtaining, or the opportunity of procuring, the larger memoirs of the eminent prelate to whom it relates. It has the particular merit of much pointedness and simplicity of style.—*Episcopal Recorder.*

This volume presents the same characteristics as those in the series which have preceded it, being written in a style simple and lucid, yet forcible, and with evident adaptation to those for whose use it is intended.

An abridgment of a larger Memoir was issued in this country last year ; but the little book before us is designed to accomplish the same purpose in a much more happy and effective manner.—*Churchman.*

No name touches more thrillingly the chords of Missionary Life in the Church than those of Heber and Martyn; and we need not say to any of those who are familiar with Mr. Norton's other biographies, that he seizes and presents to the mind, with vivid and lively brevity, precisely those points which are most likely to kindle somewhat of the spirit of Heber in the breast of his readers.—*Church Journal.*

This is another volume in that attractive series which Mr. Norton has prepared, with such general acceptance, for the youth of the Church. It is written, like all its predecessors, with great simplicity and vigor.—*Christian Witness.*

A valuable and interesting addition to the lives of the Bishops. We can hardly imagine any species of religious literature so useful to the young as the lives of really eminent and holy men, told in a simple and truthful manner.—*Southern Episcopalian.*

Bishop Heber's Missionary Hymn is the cherished heart-possession of every Christian in our land. Here is a short, but full, graphic, and beautiful delineation of the noble and pious author of that hymn. Every one whose soul is inspired from week to week by the stirring song of the mighty Christian host—

"From Greenland's icy mountains,
From India's coral strand"—

will be eager to read this timely and fitting tribute to one of the most attractive and beautiful characters of modern history.—*Louisville Journal.*

www.ingramcontent.com/pod-product-compliance
Lightning Source LLC
LaVergne TN
LVHW021406110826
845150LV00007B/1811

* 9 7 8 1 4 2 5 5 1 2 1 0 1 *